Latino Americans in Sports, Film, Music,
305.86 MIN   34480

Mintzer, Richard

Hispanic Heritage

Hispanic Heritage

Title List

Central American Immigrants to the United States: Refugees from Unrest

Cuban Americans: Exiles from an Island Home

First Encounters Between Spain and the Americas: Two Worlds Meet

Latino Americans and Immigration Laws: Crossing the Border

Latino Americans in Sports, Film, Music, and Government: Trailblazers

Latino Arts and Their Influence on the United States: Songs, Dreams, and Dances

Latino Cuisine and Its Influence on American Foods: The Taste of Celebration

Latino Economics in the United States: Job Diversity

Latino Folklore and Culture: Stories of Family, Traditions of Pride

Latino Migrant Workers: America's Harvesters

Latinos Today: Facts and Figures

The Latino Religious Experience: People of Faith and Vision

Mexican Americans' Role in the United States: A History of Pride, A Future of Hope

Puerto Ricans' History and Promise: Americans Who Cannot Vote

South America's Immigrants to the United States: The Flight from Turmoil

The Story of Latino Civil Rights: Fighting for Justice

Latino Americans in Sports, Film, Music, and Government

Trailblazers

by Richard Mintzer

Mason Crest Publishers

Philadelphia

Mason Crest Publishers Inc.

370 Reed Road

Broomall, Pennsylvania 19008

(866) MCP-BOOK (toll free)

First printing

1 2 3 4 5 6 7 8 9 10

Library of Congress Cataloging-in-Publication Data

Mintzer, Richard.

Latino Americans in sports, film, music, and government : trailblazers / by Rich Mintzer.

p. cm. — (Hispanic heritage)

Includes bibliographical references and index.

Audience: Grades 9–12.

ISBN 1-59084-936-1 ISBN 1-59084-924-8

1. Hispanic Americans—Biography—Juvenile literature. 2. Successful people—United States—Biography—Juvenile literature. 3. Hispanic Americans—History—Juvenile literature. I. Title. II. Hispanic heritage (Philadelphia, Pa.)

E184.S75M564 2005

305.868'073'0922—dc22

2004020086

Produced by Harding House Publishing Service, Inc., Vestal, NY.

Interior design by Dianne Hodack and MK Bassett-Harvey.

Cover design by Dianne Hodack.

Printed in the Hashemite Kingdom of Jordan.

Contents

Introduction

by José E. Limón, Ph.D.

Even before there was a United States, Hispanics were present in what would become this country. Beginning in the sixteenth century, Spanish explorers traversed North America, and their explorations encouraged settlement as early as the sixteenth century in what is now northern New Mexico and Florida, and as late as the mid-eighteenth century in what is now southern Texas and California.

Later, in the nineteenth century, following Spain's gradual withdrawal from the New World, Mexico in particular established its own distinctive presence in what is now the southwestern part of the United States, a presence reinforced in the first half of the twentieth century by substantial immigration from that country. At the close of the nineteenth century, the U.S. war with Spain brought Cuba and Puerto Rico into an interactive relationship with the United States, the latter in a special political and economic affiliation with the United States even as American power influenced the course of almost every other Latin American country.

The books in this series remind us of these historical origins, even as each explores the present reality of different Hispanic groups. Some of these books explore the contemporary social origins—what social scientists call the "push" factors—behind the accelerating Hispanic immigration to America: political instability, economic underdevelopment and crisis, environmental degradation, impoverished or wholly absent educational systems, and other circumstances contribute to many Latin Americans deciding they will be better off in the United States.

And, for the most part, they will be. The vast majority come to work and work very hard, in order to earn better wages than they would back home. They fill significant labor needs in the U.S. economy and contribute to the economy through lower consumer prices and sales taxes.

When they leave their home countries, many immigrants may initially fear that they are leaving behind vital and important aspects of their home cultures: the Spanish language, kinship ties, food, music, folklore, and the arts. But as these books also make clear, culture is a fluid thing, and these native cultures are not only brought to America, they are also replenished in the United States in fascinating and novel ways. These books further suggest to us that Hispanic groups enhance American culture as a whole.

Our country—especially the young, future leaders who will read these books—can only benefit by the fair and full knowledge these authors provide about the socio-historical origins and contemporary cultural manifestations of America's Hispanic heritage.

1

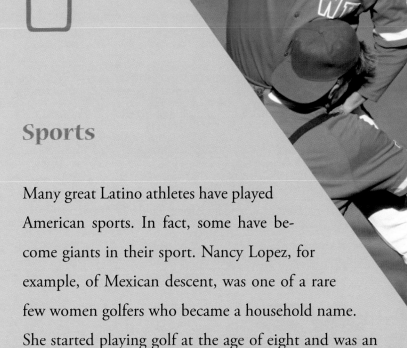

Sports

Many great Latino athletes have played American sports. In fact, some have become giants in their sport. Nancy Lopez, for example, of Mexican descent, was one of a rare few women golfers who became a household name. She started playing golf at the age of eight and was an *amateur* champion by the age of twelve. By the time she turned thirty, Nancy had made her mark on the game. She won thirty-five major tournaments and was elected to the Ladies Professional Golf Association (LPGA) Hall of Fame.

amateur: someone who does something purely for pleasure, no pay.

professional: someone who gets paid for what they do.

Boxer Oscar de la Hoya honored his Mexican heritage and American home by holding up both flags after winning the gold medal at the 1992 Olympic Games. He went on to win 223 of his 228 fights as an amateur boxer before becoming a *professional* champion. Mexican-born Anthony Munoz was also a star athlete, playing professional NFL football and being an All-Star offensive tackle in eleven out of twelve seasons with the Cincinnati Bengels before making the Professional Football Hall of Fame.

The one sport, however, that has produced the most Latino American professional athletes has been baseball. For many years, Latinos were typically not accepted in the major leagues. (African Americans faced similar prejudice.) Hispanic Americans with light skin and great talent, such as Cuban-born Lefty Gomez (a pitcher in the 1930s), were the exceptions. Others found themselves unable to crack the racial lines that divided the game. Many Latinos played in the Negro Leagues until Jackie Robinson finally broke baseball's color barrier in 1947.

From the 1960s on, baseball has grown enormously in popularity in the Dominican Republic, Puerto Rico, Mexico, and Cuba. As a result, Mexican and other leagues draw many fans and pro scouts spend a lot of their time watching the young Latino players. The impact of Latino baseball players over the past forty years has been significant and inspiring to millions of young athletes. In fact, major league baseball has made San Juan, Puerto Rico, a second home for the Montreal Expos, who play many of their games in their new "home away from home." A long list of great Latino American baseball stars includes Orlando Cepeda, Tony Perez, Jose

Cuban baseball players

scouts: experienced people who search for talent or to evaluate the opposing team.

Canseco, Miguel Tejada, and Pedro Martinez. Beyond the talents mentioned here are several true superstars, and Roberto Clemente is one of the most famous.

Roberto Clemente—Baseball Star and More

ven today, more than thirty years after his death, Latino ballplayers, especially those from Puerto Rico, will always mention the name Roberto Clemente when talking about their baseball heroes. Clemente was one of the most special players and individuals to play the game.

Born in Barrio San Anton in 1934, Roberto was the youngest of four children. As a child, he loved running and became a track and field star, winning medals for distance races and for throwing the javelin. He soon developed an interest in baseball and earned his way onto amateur teams in Puerto Rico. He had a magnificent throwing arm, great speed on the bases, and was a solid hitter. While playing for the Santurce Crabbers in the Puerto Rican Winter League, he was first noticed by the Brooklyn Dodgers *scouts*, who signed him to a contract to play for their minor league team in Montreal, Canada.

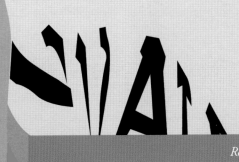

Roberto Clemente

Major and Minor Leagues

Each year major league baseball drafts the best players available to play in "the big leagues." In June of each year, the thirty clubs that make up the big leagues meet for a fifty-round draft, meaning that 1,500 players—from high school, from college, from sandlots—are selected. For most of the season, clubs like the St. Louis Cardinals and the New York Yankees can only have twenty-five players on their teams. Where do the others go?

Except for a very, very small number, most draftees will spend time in the minor leagues. The minor leagues are the training grounds for most of the stars of tomorrow. Coaches train the minor league players to perform to the level that will allow them to advance to the parent club. Unlike the major leagues, which are divided geographically, the minor leagues are divided by location and by player ability. New players may begin in the Rookie Leagues or with a single-A team. The better, more experienced players can be found on double-A teams. Just a step away from the parent club are the Triple-A teams. Not all players advance from A to AA to AAA. If he is good enough—and the parent club needs someone with his ability—a player may find himself on the fast track to the major leagues. The minor leagues are also the first stop for many future major league managers and coaches.

Other big differences between the major leagues and minor leagues include salary (minor leaguers get paid much less) and how they get from game to game. Players in the big leagues often fly. It's the bus for minor league teams.

Clemente never played for the Dodgers, however. Instead, the Pittsburgh Pirates drafted him in 1954, and it was with the Pirates that he would play for eighteen years in the major leagues. During that time, he led the National League in batting four times, played in two World Series, and won twelve Gold Glove awards for his incredible fielding. He became the pride of Puerto Rico and served as a role model for the generations of baseball players that followed.

During the winters, between baseball seasons, Clemente returned to Puerto Rico, where he met and married his wife, Vera Cristina Zabala. They had three sons, all born and raised in Puerto Rico.

Several months after Roberto Clemente finished the 1972 season by becoming one of only a few major league players to reach a career total of 3,000 base hits, a terrible earthquake struck the country of Nicaragua. Clemente was angered that medical and emergency supplies were not reaching the people who desperately needed them. On New Year's Eve 1972, he took off with a pilot in a small cargo plane loaded with medical supplies, food, and clothing to take to the victims of this devastating earthquake. His family and friends thought the trip might be too dangerous, but Clemente insisted on going; he was determined to help the victims of the terrible quake.

That was the last anyone ever saw or heard from Roberto Clemente. The plane crashed into the waters off the coast of Puerto Rico. Search teams worked around the clock, but the body of Roberto Clemente was never found. He was only thirty-eight years old, but he had already demonstrated that he was a true trailblazer, both as an athlete and as a human being. The news on January 1, 1973, shocked the people of Puerto Rico, the baseball world, and all those who knew and loved him.

By a special vote, the Baseball Hall of Fame put aside the

humanitarian: someone committed to improving the lives of other people.

usual five-year wait to be elected and voted Roberto Clemente into the hall in 1973. He was the first Latino player ever elected. Also in his honor, the Roberto Clemente Award was founded and is now given each year to the baseball player whose off the field *humanitarian* efforts are most deserving. Roberto Clemente Sports City now stands in Puerto Rico, a 300-acre sports complex with a twelve-foot statue of Clemente at the entrance. The Roberto Clemente Foundation, begun in 1993 by Roberto Jr., his oldest son, helps disadvantaged teenagers in and around the Pittsburgh area through baseball, softball, and education.

Roberto Clemente blazed a trail for others to follow. His life, on and off the playing field, provides a role model for other Latinos, and for all human beings.

Sammy Sosa: A True Rags-to-Riches Story

Sammy Sosa is one of the legends of modern-day sports. He earns multimillions of dollars and is known everywhere he goes. However, life started out very differently for the baseball superstar with the great big smile.

Sammy was born in November 12, 1968, in the Dominican Republic. His hometown of San Pedro de Macoris has become famous for producing a surprisingly large number of major league ballplayers, considering the size of the town. Kids play ball all day until the sun goes down, and as a young boy, Sammy joined the games as often as he could. Unfortunately, Sammy's

Sammy Sosa

Latino children learn to play baseball early.

dad died when he was seven, so when Sammy wasn't playing ball, he was shining shoes or doing other jobs to make money to help his mother support the family.

Baseball, as it was played in Sammy's hometown, was not the game we would recognize today. Many of the kids, including Sammy, had no money, so they turned milk cartons into gloves and used a tree branch for a bat. The ball was usually rolled-up socks with tape around them, and the fields were often not very flat. Yet, even without "proper" baseball equipment, these kids loved to play.

Sammy was fourteen before he ever picked up a real baseball bat. At that time, he started playing for fun on some of the local teams in Santo Domingo. Just two years later, a major league scout saw how well he could hit and signed him to a contract play-

Gold Glove Awards

he Silver Bat was given to each league's leading hitters. But, there was no award for the players who tried to prevent those hits. Rawlings, the maker of major league mitts, came up with the Gold Glove, and, in 1957, a gold leather glove attached to a walnut bat became the Gold Glove award. Gold Gloves are given to the most "superior fielding performance" at all infield positions and for outfield positions (they are not designated leftfield, rightfield, or centerfield for the purpose of this award). Eighteen Gold Gloves are awarded, one for each position in the National and American leagues. Managers and coaches vote on the recipients.

The most Gold Gloves ever won in a career is sixteen, by Brooks Robinson and Jim Kaat.

Gold Glove Award

ing for one of the Texas Rangers's minor league teams. Sammy gave most of his $3,500 *signing bonus* to his mother to help her and the family. He took only a couple hundred dollars to buy himself a bike.

After nearly four years in the minor leagues, Sammy was ready for the majors and the Rangers called him up to the parent club in 1989. He didn't have a very good season and was traded to the Chicago White Sox. George W. Bush, who was one of the owners of the Texas Rangers at that time, later said trading Sammy Sosa was probably the biggest mistake he ever made.

Life with the White Sox didn't go that much better for Sammy, and he was traded across town to Chicago's other team, the Cubs. That's where he became the Sammy Sosa the sports world has come to know and love. In 1998, Sosa and Mark McGwire chased the most coveted record in all of baseball, the single-season home-run record. Babe Ruth had hit sixty home runs in 1927, and thirty-four years later, Roger Maris had broken the record with sixty-one. After thirty-seven years, both McGwire and Sosa were on the way to breaking the record. By the end of the season, Sosa had hit an amazing sixty-six home runs, which would have been the most ever hit in one season, had McGwire not topped him by hitting an even more incredible seventy. Sosa, however, was voted the league's Most Valuable Player.

The rivalry of that great season made the two stars legendary. Sammy would go on to become the first player ever to hit sixty or more home runs three times. He topped five hundred home runs for his career, something that only seventeen other players had done. He has become the all-time Latino home-run champion—and he is still adding to the numbers.

On and off the field, Sammy *emulated* his baseball idol, the late Roberto Clemente. Wearing Clemente's number 21 on his back, he excelled as a player much as Clemente did. Off the field, Sammy also helped people, just as Clemente had. When Hurricane George caused great destruction in the Dominican Republic, leaving many people homeless, Sosa sent thousands of pounds of food and numerous barrels of clean drinking water to the people in need. He also helped rebuild their homes. Sosa now heads the Sammy Sosa Charitable Foundation, which over the past seven years has raised millions of dollars to help educate children and provide for families in need in the United States, the Dominican Republic, and other Latin American countries. A legendary player and future *hall-of-famer*, Sammy Sosa is loved and admired worldwide for all of his accomplishments.

signing bonus: extra money or other things given just to sign a contract to play for a particular club.

emulated: tried to equal or surpass someone by imitation.

hall-of-famer: someone who has been (or will likely be) elected to the Hall of Fame.

21

Alex Rodriguez: Baseball's Best Is a Role Model for Millions

Alex Rodriguez was born in New York City on July 27, 1975. His parents never imagined that some twenty-five years later their son would sign the biggest contract in baseball history, worth 252 million dollars.

Alex's parents, Victor and Lourdes, had married in their native land, the Dominican Republic, and moved to New York City in hopes of giving their family a better life. They opened a shoe store and were fortunate that the store did very well. However, despite their success, they longed for their homeland. So, in 1979 they packed up four-year-old Alex and headed back to the Dominican Republic, leaving relatives to run the business.

The Dominican Republic has had a great passion for baseball for a long time and many major leaguers have come from the small towns where baseball is played day in and day out on rugged fields. Alex Rodriguez, however, had only a few years of playing ball in the land of his heritage. By the time he was eight, his family returned to the United States and settled in Florida, again running a shoe store.

Then, shortly after he turned nine, Alex's life changed. His father left the house one evening, never to return. His older brother and sister, who were grown and living on their own, returned to help their mother, who held down two jobs to provide

Alex Rodriguez

a private school education for the children. Alex, meanwhile found solace playing baseball and joined the Boys & Girls Club of Miami.

By the time he reached high school, Alex had tremendous *defensive* skills and great speed, but *offensively* he was not yet very powerful. His first year in high school, he barely made the baseball team, and during the season, he spent a lot of time sitting on the bench. However, by his second year he had grown and put on weight. The coach saw this and gave him the opportunity to play regularly. Over the next three years, he compiled incredible statistics for Westminster Christian High School, graduating in 1993 and being named the USA Baseball Junior Player of the Year. He was considered by all of the sports media to be the best young talent in the country.

Major league scouts flocked around Rodriguez, who at that time wasn't sure whether or not to sign a major league contract or go to college. Still only eighteen years old, he was under tremendous pressure to make a decision that would affect the rest of his life. He took most of the summer to make up his mind. One of the deciding factors for Alex was Hurricane Andrew, which tore through Florida causing tremendous devastation. While Alex and his family were fine, there was significant damage to his high school, making him realize that life could change so suddenly. Alex elected to bypass college and sign (for more than one million dollars) with the Seattle Mariners. He used some of the money to pay off the mortgage on his mother's house and provided her with a nest egg so that she would not have to work anymore. It was his way of saying thank you for all she had done to raise him without his father in the picture.

After a couple of years of being sent up and down between the major and the minor leagues, his career began to explode. In 1995, he belted thirty-six home runs and drove in 123 runs. Over the next eight years, he would put up amazing numbers, shattering records for a shortstop and putting himself at a pace to become the greatest home run hitter ever. He became the youngest player to hit his 350th home run and is on pace to hitting 400 home runs before the age of thirty. A perennial All-Star, he has become known as the greatest player in a game filled with outstanding talent. In 2003, he was the American League Most Valuable Player and in 2004, after playing for Seattle and Texas, he was traded to the home of his birth, New York City, to play for the New York Yankees alongside his pal Derek Jeter.

defensive: to prevent the opposing team from scoring.

offensively: in a manner that will allow your team to score.

Rodriguez showed that talent and persistence at every level would pay off. He was dedicated to baseball since the age of four and has become a role model for children in the Dominican Republic and all over the world. Inspired by Roberto Clemente and other Latino ballplayers before him, "A-Rod," as he's known, has left an *indelible* impression on athletes everywhere. He has also not forgotten who was there for him when he was devastated by the departure of his father: he works extensively with the Boys & Girls Clubs of Miami and hosts their annual fundraising dinner. A-Rod also personally donated nearly four million dollars to the University of Miami to build a stadium and fund annual scholarships for Boys & Girls Club members.

Juan Marichal: From Pitching to Politics

here was no mistaking Juan Marichal when he pitched in the major leagues. Before delivering the ball to home plate, he would kick his leg straight up, higher than his head; this became his signature pitching motion. The high-kicking star of the San Francisco Giants not only turned out to be a superstar pitcher, but in recent years, he has played an important role in bringing players from the Dominican into the minor and major leagues.

Juan Antonio Marichal was born in the Dominican Republic in October 1937, and he grew up on a farm in the small town of Laguna Verde. His father died when he was three, and times were difficult for his family. When he wasn't helping

Juan Marichal

Puerto Rican children in a baseball factory

on the farm, Juan was playing baseball, learning to become a very dominant pitcher. After serving in the Dominican Air Force, the San Francisco Giants drafted the nineteen-year-old and sent to play on one of their minor league teams.

Then, in July of 1960, Juan Marichal was called up to pitch in the major leagues. His first ever game was one of the greatest major league *debuts* in baseball history. He pitched no-hit baseball for seven innings against the Phillies. When the game ended, he had allowed just one hit in a 2-0 shutout victory. He also struck out twelve batters. Clearly, he was in the big leagues to stay.

debuts: does something for the first time.

For more than a dozen seasons, he was one of the best pitchers in baseball. Marichal, now known as the Dominican Dandy, won more than twenty games in six different seasons. The three pitchers most talked about as the greatest of their era were Sandy Koufax of the Los Angeles Dodgers, Bob Gibson of the St. Louis Cardinals, and Juan Marichal of the Giants. Many baseball fans, writers, and broadcasters debated which of the three was actually the best. When his career ended Marichal had 243 wins and was the first Latino pitcher in baseball history to throw a no-hitter.

Juan Marichal retired from baseball in 1975, and eight years later he was voted into the Baseball Hall of Fame. He might have gotten in sooner, based on his tremendous career, had it not been for one incident that haunted him for many years. In 1965, while the Giants were playing their archrivals, the Los Angeles Dodgers, the two teams came close to fighting with each other several times during the season; on this particular day, Koufax and Marichal were hooked up in a close game. Dodger catcher Johnny Roseboro wanted Koufax to throw a

29

pitch at Marichal, but when Koufax refused, Roseboro threw the ball back to the mound, and it came very close to hitting Marichal. The two got into a heated argument and suddenly the usually well-mannered Marichal did something completely out of character: he turned and hit Roseboro over the head with the bat. A massive fight ensued.

As a result of the brawl, Roseboro had a concussion, and many people in baseball wanted Marichal banned from the game for life. He received a fine and an eight-day suspension. The incident, however, followed him for the next ten years of his career. By the time Roseboro retired, however, he not only forgave Marichal, but the two had become friends. In fact, Roseboro campaigned for Marichal to be voted into the Hall of Fame.

After his career ended, Marichal was hired to scout Latin American talent for the Oakland Athletics. He spent much of his time with his family, including his six children, on his banana and rice farm in the Dominican Republic, and helped many young ballplayers develop their skills in hopes of making it to the major leagues.

Then, in 1996, Dominican president Leonel Fernández offered Juan Marichal a political position as minister of sports, physical education, and recreation. In his new political position, Marichal oversaw the building of ballparks in the Dominican Republic and played a significant role in helping major league baseball talent scouts discover Dominican talent. He was the first Latino athlete to go from the ballfield into politics. To show his loyalty to his hometown, Marichal had a stadium constructed there along with many other facilities where kids could develop their skills.

Marichal, who remains a hero in his homeland, is largely responsible for the hundred or so Latinos that are now playing on big league teams, not to mention the many young up-and-coming Dominican players who have dreams of someday making the pros. He has had a tremendous impact on sports both on and off the field.

Habla Español

atleta (aht-lay-tah): athlete

béisbol (bayees-bole): baseball

jugador (hoo-gah-door): player

Chi Chi Rodriguez:
Star on and off the Golf Course

hi Chi Rodriguez is a member of the Professional Golfers Association (PGA) International Hall of Fame. Born in Puerto Rico in 1935, Chi Chi worked in the sugarcane fields with his father. He actually started working on his golf swing at the age of six, using a branch as a club and with tin cans hammered into "golf" balls. By the time he was twelve, he had gotten a hold of some real golf equipment and become a pretty good golfer.

For the next five decades, he would continue to impress people, hitting golf shots as far as 350 yards (which was amazing for a skinny five-foot, seven-inch golfer). He represented Puerto Rico in the international golfing World Cup competition for twelve years and won many tournaments in the 1990s as a member of golf's Senior Tour, for players in their fifties and sixties. Despite a heart attack in 1998, Chi Chi refused to give up the game he loves.

Off the golf course, he started the Chi Chi Rodriguez Youth Foundation in Clearwater, Florida, which helps abused and runaway kids. Chi Chi always felt that if he could make it as a great golfer, these kids could make it, too. He is a role model for many youngsters.

Chi Chi Rodriguez

Latino Americans in Professional Football

In Latin American countries, as well as many other nations around the world, football, or futbol, refers to the game we know as soccer. American football is played in very few countries outside the United States. That, however, hasn't stopped many Latino American athletes from pursuing professional football in the National Football League (NFL). Soccer-style kickers have, for years, been very successful in American football. The Gramatica brothers, Bill and Martin, from Argentina, for example, are known as two of the best kickers in the league history. Tony Gonzalez, of Cape Verdan, is an All-Star tight end for the Kansas City Chiefs, and Jeff García was a star quarterback for the San Francisco 49ers for several years.

Among the other Latino Americans in the NFL are:

Kansas City Chiefs' kicker Jose Cortez from El Salvador

Arizona Cardinals' Chris Dishman from Mexico

Atlanta Falcons' center Roberto Garza from Mexico

Cleveland Browns' guard Joaquin Gonzalez from Cuba

Cincinnati Bengels' guard Victor Leyva from Mexico

Oakland Raiders' cornerback Paul Miranda from Honduras

Detroit Lions' guard/tackle Frank Romero from Mexico.

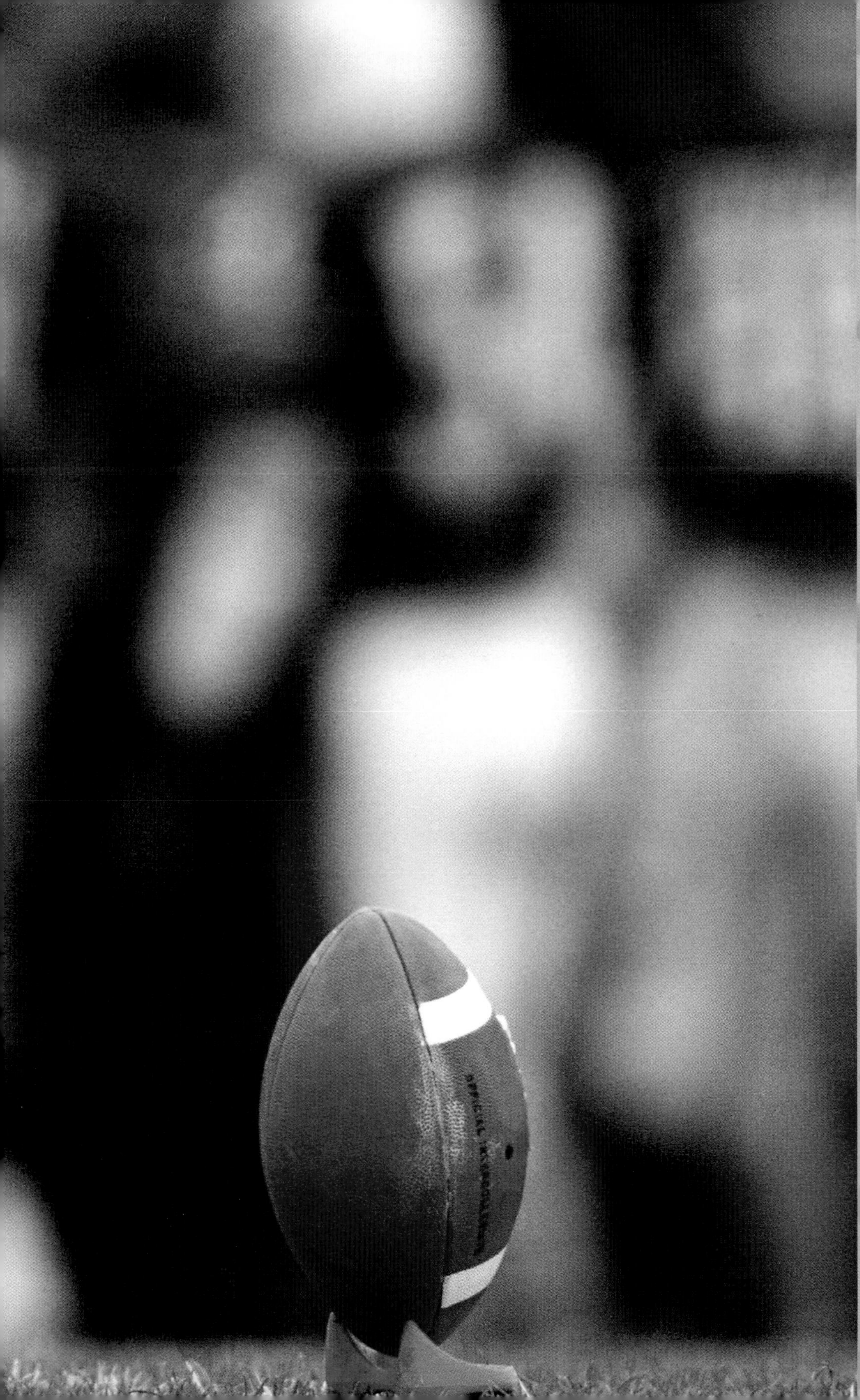

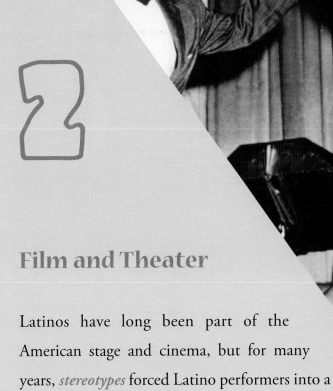

Film and Theater

Latinos have long been part of the American stage and cinema, but for many years, *stereotypes* forced Latino performers into a limited number of roles. Frustrated by being depicted in a way that was often not very positive, many performers left the United States and made movies in Mexico and other Spanish-speaking countries. Some Latino performers, however, were determined to succeed in Hollywood and worked very hard to be noticed by talent scouts.

stereotypes: opinions of someone based on generalizations and incomplete information.

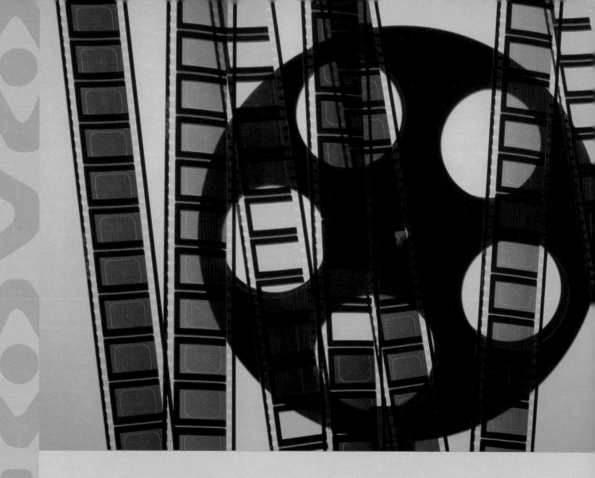

typecast: to be seen in one way, or as able to portray one type of character.

Actresses in early film needed to be graceful, attractive, and able to light up the screen with their presence. In the 1920s, silent-film star Lolita Dolores Martinez was among the first major Latino actresses to achieve American fame. She would be a star into the 1930s and the era of the talking motion pictures. Actress Rita Hayworth followed in the 1930s and '40s and was a huge favorite with male audiences because of her great beauty. Today, popular favorite Cameron Diaz continues the tradition of beautiful, talented actresses with Latino roots. While many actresses, including Rita Moreno and Chita Rivera embraced their Latin heritage, others, such as Raquel Welch (born Raquel Tejada), worked hard to hide their background, thinking it might limit their career choices.

Actors, often *typecast* in early Hollywood films as either gangsters or Latin lovers, have also made their mark in films and on the stage. Puerto Rican–born Raul Julia's career ranged from Spanish-language versions of Shakespeare's MacBeth to Gomez Addams in the Addams Family. From 1936 on, Mexican-born Antonio Quinones, better known as Anthony Quinn, established himself as one of the best-known stars of the American cinema.

Today, young and old Latino performers are continuing to star in major films and on stage in Broadway shows. Several have blazed a trail, opening up the doors to a wider range of roles for Latinos than ever before.

Chita Rivera: Legend of the Theater

roadway, which runs through the heart of Manhattan Island, is known worldwide as the theater capital. Starring in a Broadway show is one of the greatest honors for any performer. Unlike film and television, you can't make a mistake and have it edited out of the final scene, so being on stage means you have to be a confident and talented performer.

Chita Rivera became a star of the Broadway stage in the 1950s, and now, more than fifty years later, she is still regarded as one of the greatest actresses ever to grace the Great White Way (a nickname for Broadway because of the many theater marquees that light up the street at night).

Chita, born Dolores Conchita Figueroa del Rivera, is of Puerto Rican descent. Her father played clarinet and saxophone for the U.S. Navy Band. Following his death when she was seven, her mother went to work at the Pentagon. She grew up a tomboy, running with the boys and jumping up and down on the furniture in the family home in Washington, D.C.

In an effort to calm her down, or at least get her to use her energy for something construc-tive, Conchita's mother enrolled her in ballet school. At the time, her mother did not know how important that decision would be for Conchita's future.

After a few years of ballet classes, Conchita, now fifteen, was one of only two students selected to audition in New York City for the prestigious George Balanchine's School of American Ballet. Her ballet teacher went with her to the tryout and gave her some very important advice. "Stay in your lane," she told Conchita, meaning don't worry about the other dancers . . . just be yourself and do what you do best. Conchita did just that and was accepted to the nation's leading ballet school.

By 1952, Chita, as she became known, was in her first Broadway show, a play titled *Call Me Madam*. Although she was only in the chorus, her singing, good looks, and stage presence drew the attention of Broadway producers and directors. She soon appeared in significant roles in *Guys and Dolls*, *Damn Yankees*, and other major shows. Star quality was the term used to describe her.

Then in 1957, Chita Rivera made theater history as the first actress to play Anita in the classic musical *West Side Story*. The songs were difficult for Chita to learn, but she worked long and hard to get them right. The story, however, was even more difficult for her to accept. The play was about violence and prejudice and focused on two gangs, one Puerto Rican and the other American. The lines from "America," a well-known song in the show, troubled her, because they were insulting to Puerto Ricans:

Rosalia: I'll bring a TV to San Juan.
Anita: If there's current to turn on!
Rosalia: I'll give them new washing machine.
Anita: What have they got there to keep clean?

In addition, some distasteful words are used to describe the Latino characters in the play. She felt uncomfortable at first, but she decided that if people got the meaning of the show—that too many people die senselessly because of hatred and prejudice—it would serve a greater purpose.

One day before the show was about to open in Washington D.C., a story from the headlines about a Puerto Rican boy being shot and killed by another child in a playground

Chita Rivera

in New York almost brought the show to a halt. Suddenly, the show seemed all too real to members of the cast, including Chita. None of the cast knew quite what to do, but the director told them to go on stage and do the show, hoping that people would learn from it. Frightened by the headlines, but hoping the show would serve some greater purpose, Chita performed.

Professionally, her courage was rewarded. For the next four decades, Chita Rivera would land some of the biggest roles on Broadway and make history as the first Latina to appear in hit after hit. She won several Tony Awards (theater's most coveted award) and became one of the true legends of Broadway. Even a car accident in 1986, which cracked her left leg in twelve places and required eighteen screws and two braces for her to heal, did not stop her from continuing her career. It only slowed her down for a year and made her work even harder than before to regain her marvelous ability to dance. Even today, Chita Rivera still pops up on television and appears from time to time on stage.

Rivera became the first Latino American to receive the Kennedy Center Honors, given by the President of the United States to performers who have achieved a lifetime of tremendous success. Today, thousands of young dancers, including many Latinos, audition for roles on stage with hopes of being the next Chita Rivera. Hers, however, are very hard dance shoes to fill.

Andy Garcia: The Sweet Smell of Success

he boats are small and crowded and the journey is a dangerous one, but between 1959 (three years after Andres Arturo Garcia-Menendez was born) and the mid-1990s, more than 25,000 Cubans have made the trip across the choppy waters from Cuba to Florida. Less than half of the people have survived the trip. Many others were either captured by Cuban authorities or perished in the rough waters. Andy Garcia's family was among the lucky ones. They made it to Florida.

Andy Garcia

Young boys in Cuba

In January of 1959, Castro had come into power in Cuba. At first, the Cuban people supported him. However, once he took over control of the labor unions, television and radio stations, and all professional organizations, upper-class Cubans no longer trusted him. Like Robin Hood, Castro took from the rich to give to the poor. He even took over all businesses, from major corporations to small companies. The Garcia family had been affluent, but once Castro came into power they no longer had control of their business. They decided to start over again in America.

At first the United States was hard on the Garcia family, as they had basically nothing with which to begin their new lives. But through hard work, Andy's parents built up a very successful fragrance business. Andy, meanwhile, was a popular student in high school and an excellent basketball player. However, during his senior year, illnesses, including *mononucleosis* and *hepatitis*, kept him off the basketball court. The year was difficult for him and left him feeling too weak to play sports. Looking for something else to focus his attention on, he turned to acting, and the following year he attended the International University of Florida, where he studied drama.

Convinced that acting would be his future, Andy took off for Hollywood in the mid-1970s, determined to find his way into movies or television. Despite his good looks, he had a hard time finding roles, as there were not enough film parts for Latino actors. That didn't bother Andy, who had a never-give-up attitude and was driven to succeed, as his father had been when they first came to America.

He credited his father with giving him a strong work ethic. "My father always said, 'Don't ever take a step backward, not even to gain momentum.' He showed me how to be persistent and dedicated. He told me to take slow and steady steps and I would succeed. He also said that persistence is the mother of opportunity and luck."

Andy Garcia's desire to succeed would soon pay off in 1981, when he was cast as a gang member in the first episode of the popular TV series *Hill Street Blues*. From there it took a few years, but slowly his acting career took off; he began to make motion pictures and not only became a movie star but was even nominated for an Academy Award.

He also took time to marry his girlfriend of seven years; they have been married more than twenty years and have four children, three daughters and a son.

Garcia is proud of his Latino roots. In fact, he portrayed Arturo Sandoval in a special made-for-TV movie called *For Love or Country: The Arturo Sandoval Story*, a performance that earned him Emmy and Golden Globe nominations. Sandoval, who plays classical trumpet, is one of the most famous musicians in Cuban history. He eventually left Cuba to come to the United States, where he has continued to perform as well as become a university professor of

mononucleosis: an infectious disease producing swelling of the lymph nodes, sore throat, fatigue, and increased lymphocytes in the blood.

hepatitis: an inflammation of the liver causing fever, jaundice, abdominal pain, and weakness.

45

music. Garcia has both pride and compassion for Sandoval. His story touched Garcia's heart as a fellow Cuban who struggled to achieve recognition for his talents.

Garcia is a marvelous role model for young Latino performers who understand that it takes hard work and dedication to succeed—as both an actor and as a compassionate member of the human race.

Jennifer Lopez: Born to Sing and Dance

nown as "J-Lo," Jennifer Lopez has become one of the world's biggest stars, with best-selling CDs and major motion pictures to her credit. Over the past seven years, she has also become the highest-paid Latino actress of all time and the first to receive over a million dollars for a movie role.

Born in 1970 in the Bronx (New York City), Jennifer was one of three girls in her family. Her parents, both born in Puerto Rico, met after moving to the United States. Although Spanish was often spoken at home, Jennifer never learned to speak it very well. Her mother was a kindergarten teacher and her father a computer technician. She says that it was her parents' strong work ethic that made a difference in her life. They taught her to work very hard for whatever she would achieve.

As a child she loved sports, playing softball and tennis and doing gymnastics. But as she got older, performing was what she

Jennifer Lopez

really loved. She began taking singing and dancing classes at the age of five and was inspired by seeing the play *West Side Story*, starring Rita Moreno, who was one of the most successful Latino actresses of all time.

As a teenager, Jennifer starred in musical theater and continued taking dance classes. While her mother enjoyed watching her daughter perform, around this time her mother began having doubts about Jennifer making it in such a tough industry as show business. Jennifer, however, was determined to succeed and moved out of the house at the age of eighteen. She later told a magazine reporter that when she called home looking for support after a failed audition, her mother would say, "Don't you ever call me crying again! You wanted to be in this business, so you better toughen up!" Jennifer did just that. She moved to Los Angeles and kept going on auditions.

A casting call for dancers to be part of a Fox comedy series changed Jennifer's career. She was hired as a "Fly Girl" in 1990, which was what they called the dancers on *In Living Color*. From there, she landed several TV roles over the next few years and even parts in the movies *Money Train* and *My Family: Mi Familia*. The producers of these films helped Jennifer get the most important role of her career. In 1997, she starred in the movie *Selena*.

Selena Quintanilla Perez was a young Latino singer who was murdered in 1995. By her early twenties, Selena had become a legend in parts of Mexico, throughout much of Texas, and in the hearts of many Latin Americans. She was preparing to do her first English-language recording in hopes of following in the footsteps of Gloria Estefan as a crossover superstar, when she was suddenly gunned down by the president of her fan club.

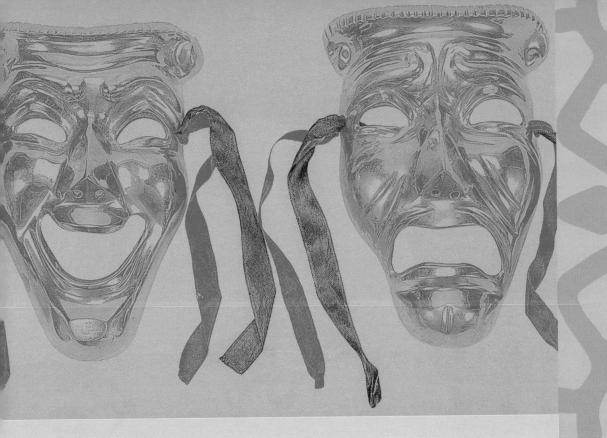

Jennifer was a hit in the movie, and the music in the film rejuvenated her desire to sing. She has since had three very successful CDs and plenty of popular music videos. When her movie *The Wedding Planner* hit number one on the film charts, she also had a number-one best-selling CD, becoming the first singer to top both the film and music charts the same week.

Since the late 1990s, Jennifer Lopez's career has skyrocketed. She has won many awards, including a World Music Award as the World's Best-Selling Latin Female Artist in 2002. She has also started her own fashion line, opened a Cuban restaurant, and has her name associated with two perfumes. From her humble beginnings in a small house in the Bronx, she now owns a $9 million home in Florida. But beyond the awards, the new business ventures, and the many articles and photos of J-Lo that appear in magazines every week, she remains an inspiration not only to Latino performers, but to all up-and-comers who realize that by working hard—and staying determined—one can reach even the most lofty goals.

Ricardo Montalban

Ricardo Montalban: The Elder Statesman of Latino Performers

choreographed:
planned out a dance
routine.

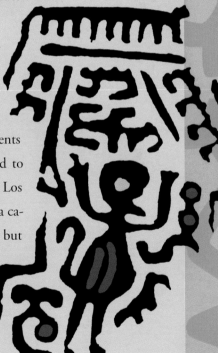

ou may not know him by name, but you've probably seen or heard Ricardo Montalban many times in movies and on television shows. He has appeared in nearly a hundred films and has either starred in, or been a guest on, more than fifty television shows. Now over eighty years old, he continues a career that has spanned seven decades.

Born in 1920 in Mexico City, Montalban enjoyed a happy childhood. His parents were of Spanish descent, and the young Montalban dreamed of growing up to be a bullfighter. However, when his brother took off for Los Angeles, Ricardo wanted to go along. He promised his parents he would finish high school once he got there; he learned to speak and write English while completing high school in Los Angeles. In LA, he became interested in acting. He started a career that immediately led to small roles in motion pictures, but he did not stay in LA long. His mother became ill, and Ricardo returned to Mexico.

While he was back in Mexico, Montalban made several Spanish-speaking films and even attracted the attention of an American talent scout. When he returned to the United States, he was cast in more interesting roles, including some films with Olympic swimmer Esther Williams, who made several very popular musicals featuring her in the swimming pool with many swimmers doing *choreographed* rou-

Montalban is a skilled swimmer.

synchronized: done at the same time.

tines, acts that were similar to the modern *synchronized* swimming you see at the Olympics.

During his sixty-three years in show business, Montalban has playing a variety of roles and has been seen in many different types of films, including one of the *Planet of the Apes* movies, *Star Trek II, The Wrath of Khan,* and two of the recent *Spy Kids* movies. Montalban proved that an actor of any ethnic heritage could play many different roles. In fact, he even played a Japanese man in the movie *Sayonara.*

It was his television role as Mr. Rourke on *Fantasy Island* that drew more attention than any of his films or his many commercials for Chrysler cars. On Fantasy Island he played a millionaire who allowed people come to his private island to make their fantasies come true. Sometimes the fantasies were wonderful; other times they didn't work out as planned. The hit series lasted six years and lives on in reruns. His television credits continue even today, as he is heard on Disney's animated hit series *Kim Possible* as the voice of the notorious villain Senior, Senior.

Montalban did not let his personal success get in the way of his helping other Latino performers. In 1970, he founded an organization called Nosotros, with the hopes of improving the way in which Latinos were portrayed in films. Nosotros campaigned to show that Latinos should not be stereotyped and instead should be able to have the same wide range of roles that Montalban enjoyed in his career. The organization also began seeking out young Latino performers and helped train them, not only as actors, but also for off-camera jobs such as directing and producing. His support for his fellow Latinos over the past thirty-some years has opened the door for many young Latinos and Latinas to make their way into the industry.

Habla Español

premios (pray-me-ohs): awards

peliculas (pay-lee-coo-lahs): films

nosotros (no-so-trose): us

Jose Ferrer

And the Oscar Goes to ...

In 1950, Puerto Rican–born Jose Ferrer won the Best Actor Oscar award for his role in the movie *Cyrano De Bergerac*. He was nominated again two years later. Mexican-born actor Anthony Quinn won two Oscars for Best Supporting Actor, first in 1952 for his role in *Viva Zapata!* and then for his portrayal of artist Paul Gauguin in the movie *Lust for Life* in 1956. He was also nominated twice for Best Actor awards but did not win. Mexican American actor Edward James Olmos was nominated for Best Actor in 1988 for his role in the film *Stand and Deliver*.

To date, no Latina actresses have won a Best Actress award. However, Mexican-born Salma Hayek was nominated for her role in the movie *Frida* in 2002. The popular, talented, and beautiful Hayek hopes to become the first Latina actress to win the prestigious award.

3

Television

In the early days of television, few minorities were seen in featured roles. Latino characters made occasional appearances on situation comedies (sitcoms), typically as gardeners or as some other type of domestic help. Prejudice and stereotyping was evident on the small screen.

Desi Arnaz

Desi Arnaz: Lucy's "Other Half"

ne of the few exceptions was Desi Arnaz who played Ricky Ricardo, the Cuban-born bandleader husband of Lucille Ball on one of television's all-time most popular shows, *I Love Lucy*. In real life, they were also husband and wife.

Lucille Ball was a natural for television. She was an attractive and extremely funny performer who was well known through her film roles. When it came time to plan the television show in the early 1950s, Lucy had to fight with the network executives to let Desi be her on-camera husband. The network executives were concerned that the American public would not like Desi's Latino accent. How wrong they were. Ricky became a huge hit, and along with Lucy and their lovable neighbors, Fred and Ethel, they created a show that after nearly fifty years is still as funny as ever.

Desi Arnaz brought new ideas to television. One of his many successful ideas was the use of two cameras on the show, which meant that the audience at home could get two different views of the people talking by switching back and forth between the cameras. This is used today in all shows, so most viewers are unaware of the importance of the two-camera concept created by Desi Arnaz.

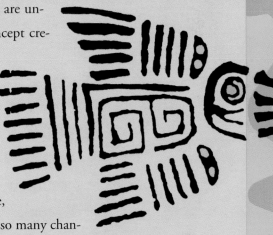

Over the decades that followed, few Latino performers were able to make an impact on network television. Without someone like Lucille Ball to fight for them, Latinos were simply not getting prime-time programs. Telemundo and other networks were, therefore, created to air Latino programming. Today, with so many channels available, Latinos are finally able to get more television exposure than ever before. The young talents look at the trails blazed by a few Latinos who have worked long and hard to create such opportunities.

war correspondent: a reporter who covers war from the battlefield.

Geraldo Rivera: Making Strides in Broadcasting

rior to the war in Afghanistan, journalist, reporter, and talk show host Geraldo Rivera joined Fox News Network as a *war correspondent* in November of 2001. This would open yet another chapter in what has now become a remarkable thirty-two-year career in broadcasting.

Rivera's father was of Puerto Rican descent and his mother was Jewish. Proud of both heritages, he grew up in New York City as a Puerto Rican Jew. After graduating high school, he left New York to attended college in Arizona before returning to Brooklyn to attend law school. Instead of law, however, he was drawn to broadcasting and decided to pursue the busy life of a television reporter. There were few Latino reporters at English-speaking stations, but Rivera was not to be denied his opportunity. At every station where Rivera worked, he proved that by digging for good stories, he could win acceptance and respect.

Finally, as a reporter for WABC-TV in New York, he first gained widespread recognition with a series of reports he did on Willowbrook, a hospital for the mentally ill. The conditions inside the hospital were disgusting and nothing was being done about it. He exposed the dirty, unsanitary conditions on television, and the government began an investigation that ended with the closing of the hospital. For his work, Rivera received broadcasting awards and the respect of the news media, a hard group to win over.

Geraldo Rivera

61

syndicated: sold television programs directly to independent stations rather than through the networks.

Geraldo's hard work as a reporter and on-camera popularity earned him a job on ABC's popular show *Good Morning America*. He was the first Latino on a national network news program, and he soon became the first Latino on a primetime news magazine show when he was asked to join *20/20*. From there, Rivera went on to have his own *syndicated* show, featuring stories that ranged from hard-hitting news to entertaining and even bizarre stories.

Throughout his career, he has often been involved in major stories. He was the first to broadcast on television the film of the assassination of John F. Kennedy, and his report on drug use by Elvis Presley was one of the highest rated *20/20* broadcasts. A special on the conditions and activities of women in prison won him awards, and his syndicated special on the opening of gangster Al Capone's vault also drew a record number of viewers.

Unfortunately for Geraldo, the vault was empty and he took a great deal of ribbing for several years.

As a foreign correspondent, he travels to countries around the world. Often this includes covering wars, which has put him in many dangerous situations. He has been on, or near, the front lines in Guatemala, the Philippines, and Nicaragua, as well as the ethnic conflicts in Croatia, Bosnia, and Kosovo. Most recently, he has gone to Afghanistan and Iraq.

His 170 awards for journalism are a tribute to his hard work and his neverending quest to report stories. His audience has crossed ethnic, religious, and cultural boundaries, and as a result, it has opened doors for Latino reporters worldwide.

Maria Hinojosa

aria Hinojosa is a correspondent for CNN, the host of a public affairs program on NPR, and an author.

Maria was born in Mexico City, Mexico, and grew up in Chicago. She broke into broadcasting as a producer and host of a Latino radio show while attending Barnard College in New York City. At Barnard Maria majored in Latin American studies, political economy, and women's studies. She joined NPR in 1985, and worked as a general assignment reporter for six years. She also hosted a public radio affairs talk show in WNBC-TV in New York. Her involvement with NPR continues with her hosting of Latino USA, a weekly program reporting on news and cultural events in the Latino community.

In May 1977, Maria joined CNN as a correspondent. She became the first correspondent responsible for reporting on urban affairs. She has reported on the September 11, 2001, terrorist attacks, the space shuttle Columbia crash, and the struggle of Kosovar Albanians in the United States. In 2001, she was the first Mexican American to write a column for *Time* magazine.

Maria has won many awards for her work—and as a mother. Today she is a frequent lecturer on the Latino community and the media.

Jim Avila

im Avila has been the most visible Hispanic network news correspondent on television since 1997. In 2001, he reported 133 stories for NBC News.

The son of a father of Lebanese descent and a Hispanic mother, Jim began his career in 1973 in San Francisco, California, on both radio and local television newscasts. He moved to Chicago in 1980. Jim first worked for ABC, CBS, and the local NBC affiliate before NBC news tapped him to be a Chicago-based correspondent for the national news in 1996. In 2000, he was made a national correspondent. As a national correspondent, Jim has covered such topics as the O. J. Simpson murder trial, September 11, 2001, terrorist attacks, the wars in Afghanistan and Iraq, and the Washington, D.C. sniper attacks. His work has earned him many awards, including an Emmy Award for his work covering the O. J. Simpson trial.

George Lopez:
A Long, Hard Climb Pays Off

or more than twenty-five years, George Lopez has been performing stand-up comedy at clubs all around the country. His sold-out shows earned him great reviews and a large following. In addition, he has performed his comedy as a guest on many television shows, recorded comedy CDs, and become well known on the radio in California. Yet, despite several tries, he was never able to get his own television show until actress Sandra Bullock stepped up and helped him get over that major hurdle. Now, he has his own hit sitcom, the *George Lopez Show.*

Growing up, Lopez was a fan of Freddie Prinze, a Hispanic comedian who achieved stardom at an early age in the 1970s as the star of the hit television series *Chico and the Man.* Prinze, whose son is now a major movie star, could not deal with the pressures of stardom and ended what looked like the start of a brilliant career by taking his own life.

Lopez, of Mexican descent, found stardom a long uphill climb. In fact, just growing up was a struggle. He was raised by his grandparents, who did not have much money and could not give George very many things. He turned to humor as a way of dealing with hard times and made jokes about his life in poverty. "Everything I couldn't have, I made jokes about," says Lopez.

George stuck with his comedy and would tell jokes to anyone who would listen. Eventually, he started going on stage at the local comedy clubs in Los Angeles. For years, he made audiences laugh talking about Taco Bell, TV commercials, cars with

George Lopez

Latino-sounding names, and anything else he could find that was funny. He was able to laugh at his heritage while still being very proud of it. But while Lopez talked about his Latino heritage, he rarely ever talked about his family or his personal life on stage. Then one day, the agent of another performer gave him some important advice, suggesting that perhaps he should get more personal in his comedy routine. Lopez took the advice and began talking on stage about his poor childhood, his parents, grandparents, and other parts of his life.

The personal life of George Lopez sparked the idea for the television show, which has several similarities to George's real life. On the show, as in real life, his character does not know his father and spends time looking for his dad. In one episode, he finds him and is able to say what he might have told his real-life dad had he met him. (Today, Lopez is married and is a dad himself.) He is proud to have the most successful Latino television hit since *Chico and the Man,* some thirty years ago.

Despite special Latino nights at comedy clubs and the tour of several Latino comics, few comic performers have been able to make it into the mainstream and get all types of audiences to appreciate their comedy. Lopez made a giant step, proving that a Latino comic can win over all types of people and have a hit television series. Young performers now look at George Lopez much as he once looked at Freddie Prinze. They see the possibilities and understand that the hard work it takes to be a successful comic can pay off with a television series.

Jimmy Smits: Opening Doors for Latino Actors

rom the hit television shows *LA Law* and *NYPD Blue* to the latest *Star Wars* epic, actor Jimmy Smits has played a wide variety of roles. He has also made many Latino American actors very proud, as they've seen him get the types of roles Latinos have rarely been able to attain. For many years Latino actors in Hollywood have been cast in roles as gangsters, drug dealers, or hot-tempered, violent characters. Jimmy Smits, however, has made an impact by portraying a prominent attorney and a detective on the New York City police force.

Born and raised in Brooklyn, New York, Smits' father was from the small South American country of Suriname, and his mother was born in Puerto Rico. His parents divorced when he was ten, leaving him as the man of the household. His mom emphasized the need to get a good education, and Jimmy worked hard in school, while playing football in his spare time. By the time he reached high school, he was a top student and a solid athlete. However, he gave up sports to focus his attention on acting. Jimmy took drama courses and continued acting during his years at Brooklyn College, but he still got his degree in education. He knew how difficult it might be to succeed as an actor, and he wanted a teaching career to fall back on.

Acting, however, remained his first love, so Smits went on to earn his master of fine arts degree in drama in 1982. Things moved quickly for the good-looking actor. While many other performers try for five to ten years to land a major part, Smits got a huge break, landing the role of Victor Sifuentes in the NBC series *LA Law* in less than four years.

During his time on *LA Law,* Smits became one of TV's hottest new stars. By the time he left the show in 1991, he had won an Emmy Award, the highest honor for a television performer. Upon returning to Brooklyn he was named the "King of Brooklyn" at the Welcome Back to Brooklyn Festival in 1991. His friends, family, and those who knew him when he grew up in Brooklyn, were especially proud of his accomplishments.

Next, Smits ventured into motion picture roles, but he didn't have the same success as he had enjoyed on television. Many of the movies he was in were not very successful, and his Latino

Jimmy Smits

heritage was winning him roles as the head of a South American illegal drug ring, a Mexican revolutionary, and a Cuban freedom fighter. But his return to television once again put him in an important role that did not focus on his Latino heritage. TV audiences loved him as Detective Bobby Simone on the hit series *NYPD Blue*. Again, Smits won several honors, including the Golden Globe Award for best television actor.

In recent years, Jimmy Smits has enjoyed more diverse film roles. He was cast as Senator Bail Organa from the planet Alderaan in *Star Wars Episode II*, and he will return in *Episode III*.

Proud of his Puerto Rican heritage, Smits is now determined to help Latino performers get more involved in Hollywood, not only as actors but as directors, producers, and writers. In 1997, he cofounded the National Hispanic Foundation for the Arts. The hope of the foundation is to see more Hispanics placed in film and television jobs. Stressing the importance of education, much as Smits learned from his mother, the foundation offers scholarships in drama, music, film, and broadcasting to Hispanic students at top universities. Leading by example, Jimmy Smits is demonstrating how education and hard work can pay off for young Latino performers.

Habla Español

noticias (no-tee-see-ahs): news

televisión (tay-lay-vee-see-own): television

educación (aid-oo-cah-see-own): education

The Alma Awards

he Alma Awards were created in 1998 to honor Latinos who are not only excellent performers in television, film, and music, but who also present positive, fair, and accurate portrayals of Latinos. The awards were actually started in 1995 as the NCLA Bravo Awards but were changed to become the Almas, which is Spanish for "spirit" or "soul," because the name best represents the determined spirit of the Latino people.

Over the years, the show has grown into a prime-time two-hour television event. The many winners include singers Gloria Estefan, Mariah Carey, Marc Anthony, Ricky Martin, Selena, comedians Paul Rodriguez and John Leguizamo, actresses Cameron Diaz, Jennifer Lopez, and Rita Moreno, actors Antonio Banderas, Ruben Blades, and Jimmy Smits, as well as Geraldo Rivera for his contributions to television broadcasting.

Latino Comic Paul Rodriguez Succeeds on Camera and Behind the Scenes

Comedian Paul Rodriguez has been performing stand-up comedy for more than twenty years. He has appeared on many television shows, including The Newlywed Game, on which he was the host; *Trial & Error*, a sitcom in which he starred in 1989; and the *Alma Awards*, which he has hosted. Rodriguez, whose son is a professional skateboarder, has also made an impact behind the scenes, writing, directing, and producing television shows. Proud of his heritage, he helps raise money for the Hispanic Scholarship Fund, which allows students to get the college education they need to succeed.

Music

Latino music has had quite an influence on American songs. From Latin Jazz to the Big Band sound of the 1930s and '40s, the infectious rhythms have had dancers moving on dance floors in clubs and ballrooms all over the country for many years. The Cha Cha, Mambo, and several other popular dances have all been the result of this popular sound.

Many different sounds and styles characterize Latino music. José Feliciano, for example, a legendary guitar player, introduced his own acoustic sound in the 1970s and stirred up controversy with his unique version of the "National Anthem." Once the controversy settled, the Puerto Rican–born Feliciano went on to win six Grammy Awards and release over sixty albums. And Santana mixed the Latin sound with rock to produce their own style Latin-Rock. They recorded a classic song by big-band leader Tito Puente called "Oye Como Va," which made its way to the rock stations from the group's very successful album *Abraxsas*. The band Los Lobos, meanwhile, blended blues with pop music and rock to produce a string of popular albums. A cover version of the 1950s hit "La Bamba" made the band famous.

In recent years, a growing number of Latino Americans have hit the charts. Some performers follow the styles of their heritage, while others, such as Mariah Carey, have emerged with a string of mainstream pop hits. Even some non-Latinos have embraced the culture, such as Madonna, who had a hit song called "La Ilse Bonita," and Jazz legend George Benson, who has used Latin rhythms on several of his albums and wrote and recorded a tune called "El Barrio."

The latest wave of Latino American music stars are reaching new heights and creating a promising future for up-and-coming Latino bands and singers, all of whom can thank the older artists described below.

Tito Puente:
The Legendary King of Latin Music

hey called him the King of Latin music. His name was Tito Puente, and for more than sixty years, he introduced Latin rhythms to the world and moved millions of people out of their seats and onto the dance floor.

Tito was born on April 20, 1923, in the East Harlem section of New York City. His parents, Ernesto Puente Sr. and Ercilia Ortiz were of Puerto Rican descent. By the age of

Tito Puente playing the timbales at the Palladium

five, he was already entering local dance contests, and by the time he reached twelve, he was playing in local Latin bands. Music came easily to Tito, and he loved to play whenever and wherever he had the opportunity.

When he was nineteen years old, he was drafted into the U.S. Navy, where he would

serve for three years. In 1945, he received his discharge and a presidential commendation for being in nine battles during World War II. Following the navy, Tito was accepted into the prestigious Julliard School of Music where he received formal training.

Throughout the 1940s and '50s, he rattled off hit after hit, while making the Mambo the hottest dance craze in the nation. Puente loved creating music that made everyone want to get up and dance. His passion for dance was clear on many of his hit albums such as *Cuban Carnival* and *Dance Mania*. During the Mambo craze of the late 1950s, Tito took part in a contest against the Mambo King, Perez Prado. The public voted for their favorite band, and Puente's band won, officially earning him the title as the King of Latin Music.

By the late '50s, his sound was known worldwide. Mambo-mania attracted the attention of all sorts of celebrities, from movie stars to athletes to politicians, who would come to see Tito and his band in action at sold out concerts. Despite not being Cuban, he received a special invitation to come to Cuba and join the celebration of fifty years of Cuban music.

During the next three decades, Puente received numerous honors and awards, including Grammy Awards for his music, keys to the city in New York and Los Angeles, and even a special award from the President of the United States. He appeared on the hit series *The Cosby Show,* thanks to one of his biggest fans, Bill Cosby.

By 1991, having now moved on to Latin Jazz, Puente released his hundredth album, which was celebrated with numerous newspaper and magazine articles. He was given a star on the famous Hollywood Walk of Fame, where major celebrities are honored with gold stars bearing their name on the sidewalk.

The music of Tito Puente served as an inspiration to thousands of young dancers and musicians. He introduced the Latino sound to millions of people worldwide. But more significant, his music brought together all types of people from many different races, religions, and nationalities. People forgot their differences and would turn out to hear Tito play. For making such a significant social and cultural impact, he became known as a goodwill ambassador, spreading his music and good feelings wherever he went.

multiple sclerosis: a progressive disease of the nervous system.

Gloria Estefan: Through Adversity to Stardom

op star Gloria Estefan was born Gloria Farjado in Havana, Cuba, in 1957. Two years later, her family would pack up their belongings, and like so many wealthy Cuban families, flee to the United States.

While Gloria was growing up in Florida, her father became a proud member of the United States Armed Forces and went to fight in the Vietnam War. During the war, he came in contact with dangerous chemicals that would leave him with *multiple sclerosis.* Life was difficult for Gloria's family and she grew up in poverty.

To make her life a little brighter, as a young child Gloria learned to play the guitar and practiced singing as often as she could. By the time she was a teenager, her vocal skills were strong, and a friend of hers invited Gloria to sing at her wedding. The wedding band, the Miami Latin Boys, listened closely as the beautiful eighteen-year-old took the microphone and started to sing. The group's leader, Emilio Estefan, not only fell in love with her voice, but he soon fell in love with Gloria. She joined the band and a few years later, the two were married.

Gloria Estefan

While she enjoyed singing every weekend with the band, Gloria remained uncertain as to whether the band could ever "make it big" in the music business. She, therefore, chose to attend Miami University and major in psychology. Music, however, was what she wanted to pursue. In the early 1980s, the band, now with Gloria as their lead singer, became very popular with Latino audiences in southern Florida. Now known as Miami Sound Machine, they signed a record deal and released a couple of Spanish albums, which were big hits. Their upbeat dance music and marvelous lead singer attracted Epic records to sign them to a recording contract to do an album in English. Sure enough, the album, called *Eyes of Innocence,* was the start of a string of hits, and the group took off. They were instantly received by English-speaking, Anglo audiences and built a major crossover following. Soon, their music was played not only in the Latino clubs but on all the pop radio stations and in all the dance clubs as well.

Several hit songs emerged from their best-selling albums, including "Congo," "The Rhythm Is Going to Get You," and "Anything for You." By the start of the 1990s, Gloria was a major pop star and decided to go solo. Usually, going solo means leaving the group. However, in this case, it simply meant making Gloria the focus of attention, while the band remained happy to continue playing behind her.

By 1991, Gloria Estefan had all you could ask for, including her first child and a long list of concert dates on her upcoming tour. Then, in one horrifying moment, everything changed. A semi tractor-trailer truck collided with the tour bus carrying Gloria and the band as they traveled along a major highway in

Pennsylvania. Gloria's back was broken, and she sustained numerous other injuries. She was listed in critical condition as the hospital staff worked for hours to close her cuts with some four hundred stitches. She lay on the operating table as titanium metal rods were inserted into her back, and she remained in her hospital bed for many months. Flowers and get-well cards poured in from all over the country and from many nations, all in hopes that she would recover from the terrible accident.

Then, as if by a miracle, Gloria was not only walking again but back on stage singing in less than one year. She had survived and returned to do what she loved the most—sing. In recent years, Gloria's career has reached new heights. She recorded albums in both English and Spanish, won three Grammy Awards, one Latin Grammy Award, recorded the theme for the 1996 Summer Olympics and was nominated for an Academy Award for the title song from the movie *Music from My Heart.* Recently, she topped off a seven-night stint in Las Vegas by recording the album *Unwrapped* from her vibrant performances.

From poverty, through a nearly fatal tragedy, and back, Gloria Estefan has been a true survivor. Selling more than 70 million records, she has become one of the most successful, best-loved Latin American crossover artists in history. Despite fame and fortune, neither Gloria nor Emilio Estefan have ever lost sight of where they came from.

When Hurricane Andrew slammed into Dade County, Florida, Gloria toured the area. "It was almost like they dropped the bomb. It's what I imagine people feel like in a war-torn city," recalled Gloria. The devastation brought her to tears. She immediately wrote a $100,000 check to the United Way's Hurricane

Relief Fund. But that wasn't enough for Gloria; she wanted to do more—and she did. She spent September 1, 1992, her thirty-fifth birthday, handing out food to hundreds of hurricane victims living in temporary shelters throughout the devastated area. She was later quoted as saying, "It was the best birthday in my life."

Ricky Martin: Leading the New Wave of Latino American Superstars

He started at the age of twelve as part of the world's most popular boy band and, over the next twenty years, became an international superstar, with sold-out concerts worldwide, millions of album sales, and plenty of awards.

Ricky (Enrique) Martin IV was born on Christmas Eve of 1971, in San Juan, Puerto Rico. The son of a psychologist and an accountant, Martin always enjoyed performing and took every opportunity to sing and act, whether it meant street performing, singing in the school choir, or taking part in a school play. From early on, everyone could see how talented he was and how likable he was as a performer. He had an instant appeal, and as a young child, he appeared in several television commercials.

When auditions were held for the young Latino boy group Menudo, Ricky was ready to launch his show business career. Menudo, formed originally in 1977, consisted of boys ages ten

Fans at a Latino concert

Ricky Martin

through sixteen; it sold over 20 million albums in English and Spanish worldwide. Unlike other boy bands, Menudo had a policy where boys would outgrow the group and be replaced, through auditions, by new members. In 1982, they had openings for several new members, and Ricky showed up. Unfortunately, he was too young and too short. Two years later, however, he returned and passed the audition with flying colors.

By 1989, Ricky was getting anxious to go out on his own and have a solo career. Having left Menudo, he took off for New York City with dreams of making it big on his own. However, after a year of unemployment, he decided that maybe he'd be better off pursuing acting for the time being and let his singing career wait. He headed to Mexico in hopes of once again getting his career started. While in Mexico, he was cast in a Mexican soap opera, which gave him steady work. As a regular actor on a popular show, he gained a following and soon returned to his music. A Spanish record label signed Ricky, and within three years he had two Spanish albums, each of which was a major hit in several countries.

Having become a very successful singer, Ricky packed up and moved once more. This time, he headed to Los Angeles, where, in 1995, he recorded his third Spanish-language album, *Medio Vivir*. This album combined Latino rhythms with rock music. Meanwhile, Ricky was still busy acting, landing a role on the American soap opera *General Hospital.*

Both his singing and acting careers throughout the rest of the '90s continued to take off. He won Latin Grammy Awards for his music and spent a year in the Broadway hit show Les Miserables. In addition, Martin recorded his fourth Spanish-language album, which sold some 20 million copies. He followed it with his first English album.

Today, Ricky Martin is a household name, known to audiences around the world. His Latin Grammy Award–winning hit "Livin' la Vida Loca" became one of the biggest international hits of all time. His mix of Latino rhythms with pop and rock has ignited a trend of young Latino performers who are experimenting with different styles. As these performers begin to gain greater fame, Martin remains at the forefront of this new wave of Latino talent. He also remains very aware of his Puerto Rican roots. In fact, he turned down an opportunity to co-star with Jennifer Lopez in a remake of the classic *West Side Story* because he did not like the way the story portrays Puerto Ricans.

Christina Aguilera: The Pop Superstar Who Owes It All to Mickey Mouse

Christina Aguilera was born in Staten Island, New York. Her mom was a talented violinist who had played in a symphony orchestra as a teenager. Her dad, originally from Ecuador, had come to the United States to join the military. As is often the case with the families of military personnel, her family moved around a lot. As a result, Christina spent her early years living in several places, including Florida, Texas, and even

Christina Aguilera

phonetically: based on the sounds of human speech.

Japan, before settling in her mother's hometown of Pittsburgh, Pennsylvania, after her parents got divorced.

By the age of seven, Christina was clearly an excellent singer. She passed an audition for the television program *Star Search,* where new talent was discovered. She appeared on the show singing a song made popular by Whitney Houston called "The Greatest Love of All." Even though she didn't win, she impressed a lot of people. In fact, by the time she was nine, she was regularly asked to sing the "National Anthem" at Pittsburgh Steelers football games and Pittsburgh Penguins hockey games.

In 1993, at the age of twelve, Christina was asked to join the Disney series, *The New Mickey Mouse Club,* a show she had auditioned for two years earlier but did not make because she was then too young. The original *Mickey Mouse Club* was a big hit show for three years in the mid-1950s. After many years, Disney brought it back for a new generation of kids to enjoy the singing and dancing of young performers. Among the young actors co-starring with Christina on the series were Britney Spears and Justin Timberlake.

Although the program was cancelled in 1994, and Christina returned to school in Pittsburgh, she had tasted stardom; she was determined to continue her singing and dancing career. Her high school classmates made life hard for her, teasing her and treating her badly, so she was forced to have home tutoring. Christina didn't mind, because she knew it was just a matter of time before she would resume her career.

Thanks to Disney, her career did resume. She recorded a song called "Reflections" for the movie *Mulan.* Although the song was not a big hit, it was popular enough to draw attention back to Christina, who went into the studio later that year, at the age of seventeen, and recorded her first album. And the rest is history.

Her first album sold over 8 million copies and featured the hits "Genie in a Bottle," "Come on Over, Baby" and "What a Girl Wants." By the age of eighteen, she was already a pop star and a three-time Grammy Award winner.

Despite her busy schedule, which already included touring to promote the album, she wanted to do something special to connect with her father's Latino side of her family. She went back into the studio and recorded a Spanish album called *Mi Reflejo*. Although she didn't speak Spanish, Christina was able to record the album *phonetically*. It sold 3 million copies and won her a large Latino following, as well as a Latin Grammy Award.

Then, to showcase the beauty of her voice and her love for the holiday, Christina recorded an album of Christmas favorites. By the time she was twenty-four, she had had two more hit albums, several pop hit songs, her own TV special, and appeared in numerous magazines.

Christina has remained true to herself and her heritage by supporting causes in which she believes. For example, she wants very much to help stop domestic violence, so she donated $200,000 to a shelter that helps battered and abused women. She has also taken part in the fight against breast cancer, supports Defenders of Wildlife, and is involved in other charities. Her performances can be outrageous at times, but deep down inside, Christina has a great desire to give something back and help other people.

Habla Español

musica (moo-see-cah): music

canto (con-toe): song

vida (vee-dah): life

loco (low-coh): crazy

Richie Valens

t was a very sad day in February of 1959 when the news hit radio and television that three of the hottest young rock stars in the world had died in the crash of a small plane. Buddy Holly was already a well-known pop star in the United States and Great Britain, with ten hit songs to his credit. The Big Bopper had just enjoyed his first hit record, and young Richie Valens was the hottest newcomer of his era at the age of seventeen. Together the three had sold over ten million records in 1958 and were just getting started.

Valens, born in southern California, was the first Mexican American rocker to make it big, debuting with the hit song "Come on, Let's Go." His next hit, written for his girlfriend, was called "Donna." The song sold over a million copies. He then had a hit by adding a rock-and-roll beat to a traditional Spanish song, "La Bamba," and it became not only a million-selling hit, but a classic that has been recorded several times over using the Valens' rock style. It was also the title of the 1998 movie that told the story of young Richie Valens' short rise to stardom.

In just one year, Valens had made a major impact and great things were predicted for his future. Unfortunately, it all ended on the night of that fateful flight.

Richie Valens

5

Government

While the number of Latinos living in the United States is increasing at a rapid pace, the number of Latinos in politics is still growing slowly. For many years, discrimination and prejudice kept many Latino voters away from the polls. Certain states even passed what were called poll taxes, meaning that to vote, a person had to pay a tax. This was intended to keep the poorer voters, which included many Latinos, from voting.

During the 1960s, Senator Joseph Montoya of New Mexico along with several other Mexican Americans, were elected to Congress. They worked hard to make changes for Latinos and outlawed the poll tax. This opened the door not only to more Latino voters but for more Latino-elected officials.

In addition, President Lyndon B. Johnson, of Texas, helped the Latino political cause. Texas, like Florida, California, and New Mexico, had a large Latino population, so Johnson was familiar with some of the most prominent up-and-coming Latino officials. He appointed several to high-ranking government positions during his years as President during the 1960s.

During the past two decades, the number of Latinos in government has begun to rise. From the former mayors of Miami and San Antonio, Maurice Ferre and Henry G. Cisneros, to high-ranking cabinet members, Latinos in government have made significant strides forward.

Bill Richardson: Eyes on the White House?

Since the turn of the twenty-first century, New Mexico's governor, Bill Richardson, has emerged as the most prominent Latino in politics. The chairman of the 2004 Democratic National Convention, he is generating a great deal of attention across ethnic and cultural lines and continues building a tremendous national following.

Richardson, whose mother was Latino, was born in California. However, he spent much of his childhood in Mexico

Bill Richardson

Down Syndrome: a genetic disorder characterized by a broad skull, blunt facial features, short stature, and learning difficulties.

City. During that time, he developed a passion for baseball and became quite good at it. In fact, after graduating high school, he was offered an opportunity to join the then-Kansas City Athletics minor league teams. He declined the offer and opted instead to go to Tufts University in Massachusetts, where he studied politics. While in college, he met his wife, Barbara, who attended nearby Wheaton University.

After college Bill Richardson, embarked on the long and steady career in politics. He spent fifteen years in Congress as a representative of New Mexico. He also served as U.S. ambassador to the United Nations in 1997 and, in 1998, U.S. Senate confirmed him as the Secretary of the Department of Energy.

However, Richardson stood out for more reasons than holding political office. In recognition of his concern for human rights abuses and his diplomatic work throughout the world, he was nominated four times (1995, 1997, 2000, and 2001) for the Nobel Peace Prize. He has also worked long and hard in support of the people of Puerto Rico who seek self-determination, which means fair and equal representation and privileges as United States citizens. While several thousand Puerto Ricans fight in the U.S. Army, and have for many years, these 8 million U.S. citizens are, in many ways, still treated as foreigners. They want to change that status, and Bill Richardson is working hard to help them.

In 2002, Richardson ran for governor of New Mexico and was very determined to win. In fact, on one day in September, while campaigning, he broke the 94-year-old record set by Teddy Roosevelt of shaking over 8,500 hands in an eight-hour period. The fast-moving Richardson shook over 13,000 hands in an eight-hour period, making the *Guinness Book of World Records*. More important, he won—by a wide margin.

During his first year in office, Governor Richardson made good on his campaign promises to improve education, cut taxes, and make New Mexico safer by getting tough on drunk drivers and domestic violence. He has continued to work hard to make improvements throughout the state.

Richardson has made no secret of his Latino heritage, asking Mexican Americans, Cuban Americans, Puerto Ricans and all Latinos in the United States to become more politically minded and to vote. Clearly, he has achieved new heights for a Latino politician in the United States. Through his hard work and dedication to the Democratic Party and the people of New Mexico, Bill Richardson is an inspiration to other Latinos in politics.

Rosario Marin: Treasurer with a Heart of Gold

If you look at a dollar bill, underneath the serial number, you'll see the signature, *Rosario Marin*. She has been the Treasurer of the United States since 2001, but stepped down from that position to run for the U.S. Senate from the state of California.

Born in Mexico City, she is not only the first Latino American to become United States Treasurer, but she is the first person born outside of the United States to hold the important government position. She is also the highest-ranking Latino to serve in President George W. Bush's administration.

Rosario Marin moved from Mexico City to southern California at age fourteen, where she learned to speak English. For seven years, she juggled several different jobs while taking night classes on her way to earning a college degree from California State University in Los Angeles. Later, while working for AT&T as a public relations manager for the Hispanic market, she entered a special program at Harvard University for senior executives. The program focused on state and local government.

Meanwhile, Rosario's first son was born with *Down Syndrome*, and in her efforts to get him the best possible care and medical assistance, she learned a great deal about the many needs of people with disabilities. As she learned more, she also became very involved in helping disabled individuals. This led to her position as Chairperson of the State Council on Developmental Disabilities.

For Rosario, politics was not as much a chosen profession as it was a means to follow her heart as she worked to help others. Once she was in politics and saw the difference she could make, she went on to work for former California governor Pete Wilson, where she learned more about how the political processes worked in the state of California.

Then, in an effort to help the people of her hometown of Huntington Park be better represented, she ran for councilwoman. She went on to be elected both councilwoman and mayor of Huntington Park, where she represented the Latino community, which makes up more than 90 percent of the 85,000 people living there.

The honor of being appointed by George W. Bush as the forty-first U.S. Treasurer came in 2001. In this high-ranking political position, she oversees the U.S. Mint and the printing and engraving of all money in the United States. This explains why her name appears on all the dollar bills printed while she was Treasurer. She has also used her political position to help Latinos—and all American citizens—learn more about finances as she encouraged them to trust and use the nation's banking and credit systems.

Rosario Marin has received a great deal of attention for her accomplishments. She has had many articles written about her and appeared on the cover of several magazines, including *Hispanic Business* magazine, where she was named one of a hundred most influential Hispanics. Even as far back as 2000, she was listed as one of the "20 Up and Coming Latinas" in the *Los Angeles Business Journal*.

Rosario Marin

Cruz M. Bustamante

Rosario continues to be an inspiration not only for Latino Americans but for women and for anyone committed to a cause.

Cruz M. Bustamante: Speaking Up for All the People

In 1998, Cruz M. Bustamante proved that Latino Americans are moving into more important roles in politics. He became the Lieutenant Governor of California and the first Latino elected to a California statewide office since 1878. Just two years earlier, he had become the first Latino speaker of the California Assembly.

Cruz, born January 4, 1953, was the oldest of six children. He grew up in the small town of San Joaquin, California, where he worked in the fields when he wasn't going to school. His parents taught him how important it was to work hard, and his dad set an example, sometimes holding two or even three jobs to earn enough money to support a family of eight. At first Cruz wanted to be a butcher, but as he grew older, his dreams changed, and he wanted to become a doctor. However, when he spent one summer doing a college internship in Washington D.C., working for a congressman, he began to take an interest in politics.

He learned how government worked and read letters from people who wanted to see changes made or receive much-needed help. As he tried to help people, he realized that politics was what he wanted to do. "I loved helping to make government work for people. I found out I was a lot better at cutting red tape

summits: top-level
conferences.

than I was at cutting meat," joked Cruz about his internship in the government.

For years, Cruz Bustamante worked in politics, helping congressmen and assemblymen, until finally in 1993, at the age of forty, he was elected as an assemblyman. He gained a lot of support as a Democrat and helped encourage Latino Americans to get out and vote. After his early years as an assemblyman, he stepped into his role as Lieutenant Governor of California. As Lieutenant Governor, Cruz has focused on improving education, saving the environment, providing people with health care, and protecting consumers from being ripped off.

Bustamante is determined to make an impact on the education of the students of California, from preschool through college. He helped lower the tuition at California state universities, wrote a law that provided a billion dollars to buy new updated textbooks for all schoolchildren, and reduced the class size in California schools. He has held education *summits* where leaders in business, education, and government meet to create a plan to get more money for better education.

When a reporter asked Cruz Bustamante if he had an "ethnic agenda," meaning that he had plans for certain ethnic groups, he responded that his plans were for people of all backgrounds—and they included decent jobs and safe neighborhoods. A father of three and grandfather of two, Cruz Bustamante has risen from the fields of central California to a high-ranking state office. Hs has inspired other Latino Americans to get involved in politics and take a stand on issues that affect everyone.

Political Firsts

hree states with large Latino populations—Florida, New Mexico, and California—were the first to send Latin American representatives to the U.S. Congress.

Joseph Marion Hernandez, born in St. Augustine, Florida, in 1793 (while it was still owned by Spain) was to become the first Hispanic U.S. representative in Congress when the territory of Florida was established in 1822. He served for only six months but opened the door for Latinos to serve in Congress.

Octaviano Larrazolo was the first Hispanic to serve in the U.S. Senate. He was born on December 7, 1859, in Allende in the Mexican state of Chihuahua. His family moved to Arizona when he was eleven. During the 1880s, he worked his way through various political positions while living in Texas. In the early 1900s, he moved to New Mexico, and by 1918, he became Governor of the state. Then, after four years in the New Mexico House of Representatives, he became the first Latin American Senator of the United States in December of 1928. Unfortunately, he took ill and died in 1930. Nonetheless, as political candidates like Rosario Marin campaign to become U.S. Senators, they owe a lot to Octaviano Larrazolo.

Timeline

1822—Joseph Marion Hernandez of Florida becomes the first Hispanic U.S. Representative.

December 1928—Octaviano Larrazolo of New Mexico becomes the first Hispanic U.S. Senator.

1947—Jackie Robinson breaks the color barrier in major league baseball.

1957—The first Gold Gloves for fielding in major league baseball are awarded.

February 3, 1959—"The Day the Music Died": Richie Valens, the Big Bopper, and Buddy Holly killed in a plane crash outside Clear Lake, Iowa.

1973—Roberto Clemente of the Pittsburgh Pirates becomes the first Latino elected to the Baseball Hall of Fame.

1992—Oscar de la Hoya wins a gold medal in boxing for the United States at the Olympic Games.

March 31, 1995—Tejano singer Selena murdered by her fan club president.

1998—Mark McGwire and Sammy Sosa break the record for the most home runs in a season.

1998—The Alma Awards are created.

August 1, 1998—Anthony Munez becomes the first Latino elected to the Professional Football Hall of Fame.

September 8, 2000—The first Latin Grammys are awarded.

2002—Jennifer Lopez becomes the first actress/singer with a movie and an album both at number one in the same week.

Further Reading

Ling, Bettina. *Jose Canseco*. Toronto, Ont.: Steck-Vaughn, 1995.

Marvis, Barbara J., and Barbara Tidman. *Famous People of Hispanic Heritage*, vols. 1–5. Hockessin, Del.: Mitchell Lane Publishers, 1996.

McCracken, Kristin. *Freddie Prinze, Jr.* New York: Scholastic Library, 2001.

New York Public Library and Alex Ochoa. *The New York Public Library Amazing Hispanic American History: A Book of Answers for Kids*, Hoboken, N.J.: John Wiley & Sons, 1998.

Perez, Frank, and Ann Weil. *Raul Julia*. Toronto, Ont.: Steck-Vaughn, 1996.

Projects Inc. Media. *Almanac of Hispanic American History*, 2 vols. Westport, Conn.: Greenwood Publishing Group, 2003.

Rodriguez, Janel. *Gloria Estefan*. Toronto, Ont.: Steck-Vaughn, 1996.

Various. *Latinos in American History*. Hockessin, Del.: Mitchell Lane Publishers, 2002.

Walker, Paul Robert. *The Life of Roberto Clemente*. Orlando, Fla.: Harcourt Brace & Company, 1991.

Zymet, Cathy Alter Alder. *Enrique Iglesias*. Langhorne, Pa.: Chelsea House, 2001.

For More Information

Hispanics in American Congress
www. loc.gov/rr/hispanic/congress

Las Culturas
www.lasculturas.com

Latino Sports Legends
www.latinosportslegends.com

American History at About.com
www.americanhistory.about.com/cs/hispanicamerican

Publisher's note:

The Web sites listed on this page were active at the time of publication. The publisher is not responsible for Web sites that have changed their addresses or discontinued operation since the date of publication. The publisher will review the Web sites and update the list upon each reprint.

Index

Picture Credits

Center for Cuban Studies: p. 11

Corbis: pp. 9, 35, 52

Dianne Hodack: pp. 6, 8, 36, 56, 74, 94

The Jesús Colón Papers, Centro de Estudios Puertorriqueños, Hunter College, CUNY, Photographer unknown: p. 37

The Justo A. Martí Photographic Collection, Centro de Estudios Puertorriqueños, Hunter College, CUNY, Photographer unknown: pp. 18, 77

Michael Whitaker: p. 44

PhotoDisc: p. 95

Photos.com: pp. 20, 24, 38, 49, 57, 63, 70, 75, 78–79, 85, 98, 103, 104

The Records of the Offices of the Government of Puerto Rico in the U.S., Centro de Estudios Puertorriqueños, Hunter College, CUNY, Photographer unknown: p. 28

Biographies

Richard Mintzer is the author of over thirty books on a wide range of topics. His background also includes writing numerous articles for national publications such as *Variety* and *The Hollywood Reporter*, for which he interviewed and profiled a cross-section of entertainers from various cultures and wrote about cinema and theater. He has also served as a writer for the educational Web site, Power To Learn (www.powertolearn.com) where he profiles the careers of people in sports and other industries for high school students to learn more about interesting career possibilities. Richard hails from New York City and is currently living with his family in Northern Westchester, New York.

Dr. José E. Limón is professor of Mexican-American Studies at the University of Texas at Austin where he has taught for twenty-five years. He has authored over forty articles and three books on Latino cultural studies and history. He lectures widely to academic audiences, civic groups, and K–12 educators.